The Amazing Adventures of BATHMAN!

by
ANDREW T. PELLETIER

illustrated by
PETER ELWELL

DUTTON CHILDREN'S BOOKS / *NEW YORK*

To Madeline,
my number 1 Bathgirl.
And to Wolfgang,
the original Bathman.
—A.T.P.

For Lucia,
Heather 'n' Becky—
my bestest friends
—P.E.

LET'S CLEAN IT UP
AMERICA —
USE SOAP!

Library of Congress Cataloging-in-Publication Data
Pelletier, Andrew Thomas.
The amazing adventures of Bathman / by Andrew Pelletier;
illustrated by Peter Elwell.—1st ed.
p.   cm.
Summary: Bathman saves Rubber Ducky
from the evil Cap'n Squeegee.
ISBN 0-525-47164-2
[1. Baths—Fiction. 2. Toys—Fiction.] I. Elwell, Peter, ill. II. Title.
PZ7.P3639Am 2005   [E]—dc22   2004021451

Published in the United States by Dutton Children's Books,
a division of Penguin Young Readers Group
345 Hudson Street, New York, New York 10014
www.penguin.com/youngreaders

DESIGNED BY
HEATHER WOOD

Manufactured in China
First Edition
1 3 5 7 9 10 8 6 4 2

It's a quiet Saturday evening around the house . . .

or so it appears.

Up in the bathroom, there's a tub full of trouble.

Thundering footsteps shake the hall.

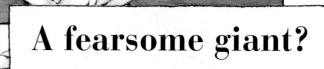

Is it a rhinoceros?

A fearsome giant?

"**Cowabunga!**" he shouts.

"*Ducky!* That birdbrain can never stay out of trouble!" says Bathman. "There's only one guy nasty enough to carry out this caper—*Cap'n Squeegee!*"

ARR!

"Cap'n Squeegee!" Bubbles, Toots, and Sham shout in fright. "He's the terror of the tub!"

Next he questions Blob the Sponge. Blob soaks up lots of news, but Bathman can't squeeze a word out of him.

And he knows better than to ask Big Moll. She always clams up tight.

Silent as the deep, swift as a stingray, the world-famous superhero slices through the suds.

Sure enough, Bathman sees the dippy duck dangling over the drain as Cap'n Squeegee laughs his fiendish laugh.

"You'll have to do better than that, my friend!" sneers Bathman. He unleashes his special Tattoo Torpedoes.

The battle ebbs and flows . . .

To celebrate, they all have
a great big bubble blast.

"Hot dog!" yells Bathman. He hops out of the tub, and Winsome wraps him in his monogrammed towel.

"See you next time, gang!" calls Bathman. "Keep your noses clean!"